MATH ADVENTURES

# TUAN TAKES A TRIP

## A TIME-TELLING ADVENTURE

by Elizabeth Everett
illustrated by Amy Zhing

GRASSHOPPER

## Tools for Parents & Teachers

Grasshopper Books enhance imagination and introduce the earliest readers to fiction with fun storylines and illustrations. The easy-to-read text supports early reading experiences with repetitive sentence patterns and sight words.

### Before Reading

- Discuss the cover illustration. What do readers see?
- Look at the picture glossary together. Discuss the words.

### Read the Book

- Read the book to the child, or have him or her read independently.
- "Walk" through the book and look at the illustrations. Who is the main character? What is happening in the story?

### After Reading

- Prompt the child to think more. Ask: Tuan tells time as he and his family take a trip to his Grandpa's house. What time do they leave? What time do they arrive?

Grasshopper Books are published by Jump!
5357 Penn Avenue South
Minneapolis, MN 55419
www.jumplibrary.com



Library of Congress Cataloging-in-Publication Data

Names: Everett, Elizabeth, author. | Zhing, Amy, illustrator.
Title: Tuan takes a trip: a time-telling adventure
by Elizabeth Everett; illustrated by Amy Zhing.
Description: Minneapolis, MN: Jump!, Inc., [2023]
Series: Math adventures
Includes index. | Audience: Ages 5–8
Identifiers: LCCN 2021970010 (print)
LCCN 2021970011 (ebook)
ISBN 9781636908731 (hardcover)
ISBN 9781636908748 (paperback)
ISBN 9781636908755 (ebook)
Subjects: LCSH: Time—Juvenile literature.
Time measurements—Juvenile literature.
Classification: LCC QB209.5 .E94 2023 (print)
LCC QB209.5 (ebook) | DDC 529—dc23/eng/20220126
LC record available at https://lccn.loc.gov/2021970010
LC ebook record available at https://lccn.loc.gov/2021970011

Editor: Jenna Gleisner
Direction and Layout: Molly Ballanger
Illustrator: Amy Zhing

Printed in the United States of America at
Corporate Graphics in North Mankato, Minnesota.

## Table of Contents

# Time for a Trip

"Rise and shine, Tuan! It is time to get ready for our trip!" says Tuan's dad.

"I can't wait!" says Tuan.
"When do we leave for the airport?"

"At 9 o'clock," says his dad.

“Is it 9 o’clock yet?” Tuan asks.

“Not yet,” says his mom. “It will be when the hour hand points to the 9 and the minute hand points to the 12.”

minute hand
hour hand
12
1
2
3
4
5
6
7
8
9
10
11

"So it is 8 o'clock now?" Tuan asks.

"That's right," his mom answers. "The minute hand needs to go all the way around the clock and back to 12. That is 60 minutes. That is one full hour. We have one hour to finish getting ready!"

Tuan packs his bag.

He watches the clock.

“It’s 9 o’clock!” he shouts.
“Let’s go!”

They drive to the airport.

"The drive took one hour!" Tuan says.

10:00

They get on the airplane at 12:00. While they fly, Tuan checks his watch.

"Look!" says Tuan. "The minute hand went halfway around the clock."

"Yes," says his dad. "Half of an hour is 30 minutes. So it is 12:30."

After they land, they wait for the train.

"When will we get to Grandpa's?" Tuan asks.

"At 3:30," his dad answers.

"That's 30 minutes from now," says Tuan. "The minute hand needs to go halfway around the clock!"

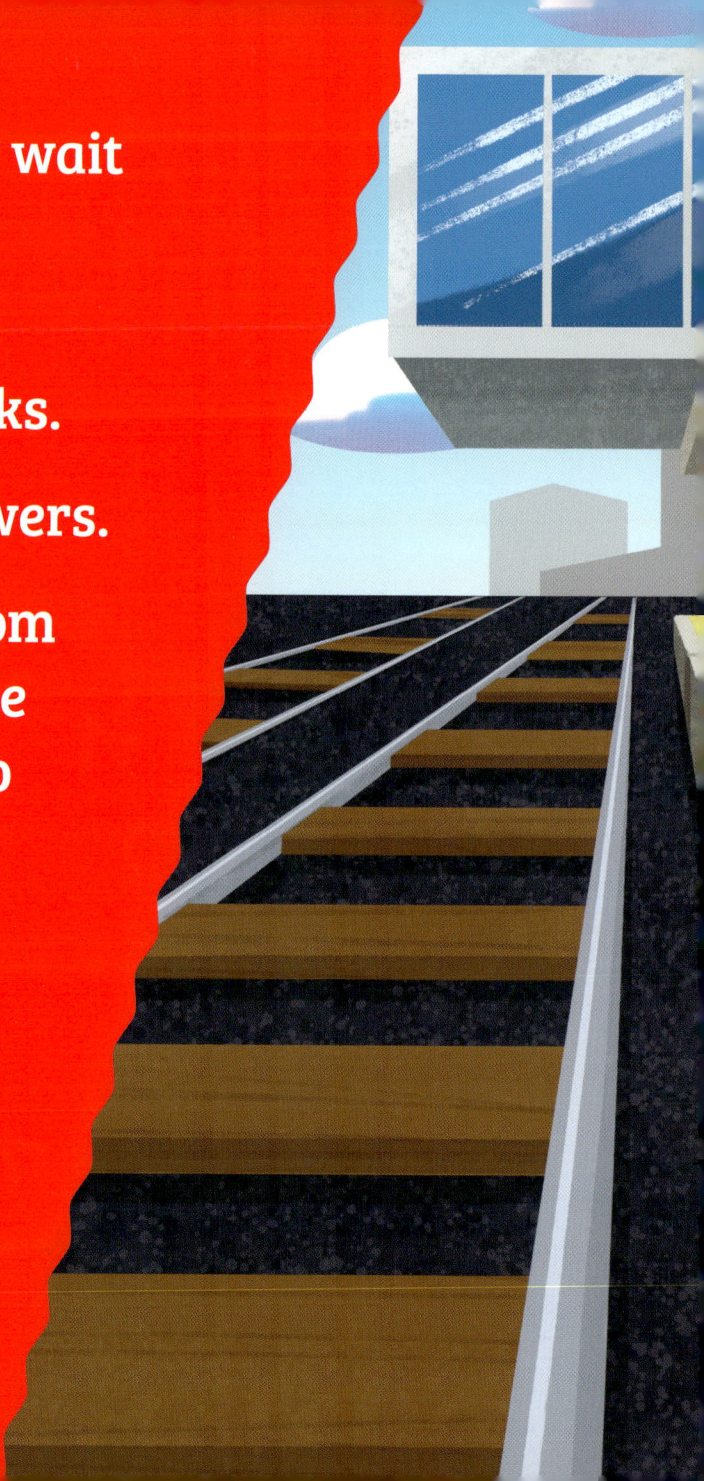

3:00

"We're almost there," says Tuan. "The minute hand is almost pointing to the 6!"

The train arrives at the station.

The walk to Grandpa's takes five minutes.

They arrive at 3:30.

"You must be tired!" says Grandpa.

"No," says Tuan. "We have time to play!"

# Let's Review!

Tuan tells time using both analog and digital clocks. How are analog and digital clocks similar? How are they different?

analog clock

digital clock

What time does each clock below read?

A.

B.

C.

D.

Let's Review! Answer Key: A. 11:00 B. 12:30 C. 4:00 D. 6:45

# Picture Glossary

**hour**
A unit of time equal to 60 minutes. There are 24 hours in one day.

**hour hand**
The short hand that marks the hours on a watch or clock.

**minute hand**
The long hand that marks the minutes on a watch or clock.

**minutes**
Units of time equal to 60 seconds. There are 60 minutes in one hour.

# Index



# To Learn More

## Finding more information is as easy as 1, 2, 3.

1. Go to www.factsurfer.com
2. Enter "**Tuantakesatrip**" into the search box.
3. Choose your book to see a list of websites.